For everyone who has ever been held captive by a book
— J. K.

For two Australian princesses, Mia and Ava
— E. E.

tiger tales
5 River Road, Suite 128, Wilton, CT 06897
Published in the United States 2019
Originally published in Great Britain 2019
by Little Tiger Press Ltd.
Text copyright © 2019 John Kelly
Illustrations copyright © 2019 Elina Ellis
ISBN-13: 978-1-68010-134-8
ISBN-10: 1-68010-134-X
Printed in China
LTP/1400/2410/0918

For more insight and activities, visit us at www.tigertalesbooks.com

Shhh!
I'm Reading!

by John Kelly • Illustrated by Elina Ellis

tiger tales

It was a wet and windy Sunday afternoon, but Bella didn't care. She was busy reading the best book EVER! And the story had just reached the AMAZING part, right near the end where . . .

"AHOY, Shipmate Bella!" bellowed Captain Bluebottom.

"It's Sunday! Are you ready for another adventure with the Windy Pirates?"

"I'm sorry, Captain," said Bella, "but today, I'd rather just sit and read my book."

"READ A BOOK?" harrumphed Bluebottom.
"BY MY SCRATCHY WHISKERS!
How could a book be better than
a voyage to Devil's Island,
a duel with Nobby
the Nasty,

and then home again
with a ship full of booty?
ARRRRRRR!"

"Well, this book is!" said Bella.
"So you can all drop anchor
and sit quietly because
I AM BUSY READING!"

Bella picked up her book
and began to read the
AMAZING part, right
near the end where . . .

"Bella, darling," squawked Maurice Penguin.

"Why aren't you ready? It's Sunday afternoon!

It's SHOWTIME!"

"Not now!" said Bella. "I'd really rather sit and read my book."

"READ A BOOK?" cried Maurice. "How could a book be more fabulous than the tippity-tap-tap of your shoes on stage, the roar of applause, and this SPANGLY costume?"

"WOW!" said Bella. "But this book is even more fabulous than ALL those sequins!"
She pointed to the band. "EVERYONE TAKE FIVE! And please be quiet, because
I AM BUSY READING!"

Bella picked up her book and turned to the AMAZING part near the end where . . .

"I claim this bedroom in the name
of the Lardon Empire!" announced
Emperor Flabulon the Wobbulous.
"NOT NOW!" exclaimed Bella.
"I'm reading this BOOK!"

"But it's Sunday!" burbled Flabulon.
"You always defend the Earth on a
Sunday afternoon."

"I know," sighed Bella. "But today,

I AM BUSY READING!"

"READING?" sputtered Flabulon.
"How could a book be more exciting than
blazing laser cannons, dodging anti-matter missiles,

and zooming dangerously fast in a really cool **SPACESHIP**?"

"WELL, THIS BOOK IS!" said Bella.
"Look, I'll save Earth after snack time!
Plop your tentacles in the corner and
BE QUIET! For the last time,
I AM BUSY READING!"

At long last, there was peace and quiet.

Bella continued to read until
she reached the end of her book,
just before snack time.

"That was the BEST BOOK EVER!"
she announced. "Now, who wants to go on
an INCREDIBLE adventure?"

Everyone looked up at her and said . . .

"Maybe later, Bella,
but right now . . .

WE ARE BUSY
READING!"